MARC BROWN

ARTHUR
MEETS THE PRESIDENT

Little, Brown and Company
Boston New York Toronto London

For my Texas friends:
Melinda Murphy, Jane Strickland, Mary Lankford,
and Nancy O'Connor

First Paperback Edition

Library of Congress Cataloging-in-Publication Data
Brown, Marc Tolon.
    Arthur meets the President / Marc Brown. — 1st ed.
       p.   cm.
    Summary: Arthur's essay wins a contest and he has to read it to the
President in a special ceremony at the White House.
    ISBN 0-316-11265-8 (hc)
    ISBN 0-316-11291-7 (pb)
    [1. Presidents — Fiction. 2. Animals — Fiction. 3. Contests —
Fiction. 4. Public speaking — Fiction.] I. Title.
PZ7.B81618 1991 Anb
[E] — dc20   90-13298

20   19   18   17   16   15   14   13   12

WOR

Published simultaneously in Canada
by Little, Brown & Company (Canada) Limited

Printed in the United States of America

"Listen carefully, class," said Mr. Ratburn. "This is a national contest, so do your best work."

"I love contests," said Muffy. "What do I win?"

"The winner visits the White House in Washington," said Mr. Ratburn.

"What do we write about?" asked Arthur.

"The subject is 'How I Can Help Make America Great,' " said Mr. Ratburn.

Everyone started writing.
Arthur started thinking.
He thought about the time he and D.W. helped
old Mrs. Tibble clean her yard.
He thought about how much more they could do
in the neighborhood if the whole class helped.
Then he began to write.

Weeks later, when Mr. Haney, the Principal,
was opening the mail his hands began to shake.
"It's a letter from the President!" he gasped.

Miss Tingley, the secretary, fainted.
Prunella, who was in the office with a stomach ache,
suddenly got better. "Open it!" she shouted.

Mr. Haney clicked on the P.A. system.
"Attention, everyone! The President of the United States
has written to announce the winner of the
'How I Can Help Make America Great' contest.
And the winner is our very own *Arthur!*
He and his class are invited to attend a special ceremony
at the White House."

Mr. Ratburn's class went wild!

"Congratulations, Arthur!" said Mr. Ratburn.
"You'll have to work hard to memorize your paper so
you can recite it to the President next Wednesday."

"Memorize . . . recite?" asked Arthur.
"Of course," said Mr. Ratburn.
"We'll all be there cheering you on."

"You're on TV!" screamed D.W. when Arthur got home.
"Listen!"

". . . he will recite his winning essay to the President and all of America," the announcer was saying.

"I feel sick," said Arthur.

"Not as sick as you'll feel when you're giving your speech," said D.W.

"There's so much to do before we leave," said Mother.
"Arthur, you'll need a new suit."
"What about me?" asked D.W.
"I need to look beautiful when *I* meet the President."
"The President is very busy," explained Father.
"He'll only have time to meet Arthur and hear him recite his essay."

"If I can remember it," said Arthur.
"Of course you can," said Father. "Just relax.
Pretend I'm the President and practice right now."
The thought of sitting next to the President made
Arthur's mind go blank.
"Ah . . . ah . . . ah," he said.
"Uh-oh," said D.W.

Monday at school everyone was busy planning the trip.
"Oh, boy! No homework for three days!" said Francine.
"Not quite," said Mr. Ratburn.
Everyone groaned.

"Each of you will have to do a report," he explained. "As we tour Washington on Wednesday, you will be our guides. So get to work. I'll see you all at the airport tomorrow morning."

Arthur tried to study his speech on the plane.
"Don't forget to mention me to the President for the
Teacher of the Year award," Mr. Ratburn reminded him.
"Aren't you excited?" asked Buster.
"I'm too nervous to be excited," said Arthur.
"You need help," said D.W.
"I'll make the speech for you.
I have a lot of ideas about how to run the country."

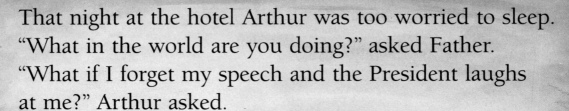

That night at the hotel Arthur was too worried to sleep.
"What in the world are you doing?" asked Father.
"What if I forget my speech and the President laughs
at me?" Arthur asked.
"The President would never laugh at you," said Father.

"Why don't you write your speech on note cards and keep them in your pocket," he suggested, "just in case." "What a great idea!" said Arthur.
He felt much better.
"Now try not to worry, and go to sleep," said Mother.

The next morning everyone met in front of the
Jefferson Memorial.
"Arthur, you look so handsome," said Francine.
"Ready to meet the President?" said Mr. Ratburn.
"I guess," said Arthur.

He reached into his pocket to make sure
the note cards were there.
"Time for your reports," called Mr. Ratburn.
"Only one more hour until we're due
at the White House."

"Our first stop is the Washington Monument, the
tallest building in Washington," explained Francine.
"Eight hundred and ninety-eight steps to the top.
Everyone ready?"
"Are you kidding?" said D.W. "I'm taking the elevator."

"This is the Capitol, where Congress makes the nation's
laws," said Sue Ellen.
"I think we all know how important it is to obey
the law," said Mr. Ratburn.

"The National Museum of Natural History has
great mummies," said Buster. "Follow me."
"No, thanks," said Muffy. "I'll meet you
at the gift shop."

The last stop was the White House.
"It's so big," said Arthur.
"Not as big as Muffy's house," said D.W.

"The White House has one hundred and thirty-two rooms,"
said the Brain. "Every President except George Washington
has lived here. It has a barber shop, clinic, indoor pool,
theater, gym, and its own library."

"And the President's office has fancy gold curtains just like the ones in *our* living room," said Muffy.
"Excuse me," said the President's secretary.
"The President is arriving.
Please follow me to the Rose Garden."

Arthur gulped.
It was almost time.
He took out his note cards.
Suddenly a strong wind blew through the garden.
"Here comes the President!" squealed Muffy.
"My speech!" gasped Arthur.
"Relax," said Mr. Ratburn, "you'll be fine."
D.W. wasn't so sure. She had a plan.

Arthur had never seen so many important-looking
people.
"Good afternoon, Mr. President," he began.
"When I think about what I can do to make America
great . . . ah, ah, ah . . ."
Arthur began to feel very warm.
His knees began to shake.
His mind went blank.
"This is the worst day of my life,"
he thought.

Suddenly Buster giggled.
Soon everyone else joined in.
Even the President was laughing.
Arthur turned bright red.
And when Arthur saw what they were
laughing at, he laughed too.

Now Arthur felt much better. He recited his whole speech without forgetting a single word. "And in conclusion," he said, "we can all help make America great by helping others."
"Good!" said D.W. "Then help me down!"